Mrs. Sullivan,
As always, I app —
your kindness and —
I hope you enjoy this
and wacky ride through
my family's "history!" !!

♡ Jessica Stacky

JESSICA STARKS & LARRY STARKS

Strolling With Stories: Tales From Horsepen

ONION PUBLISHING

First edition

Illustration by Morgan Souter
Editing by Exemplary Editing

This book was professionally typeset on Reedsy.
Find out more at reedsy.com

To my father, Larry Starks.

To my grandfather, Rufus Starks.

To My uncle, Nathaniel "Uncle Cornbread" Starks

To my great uncle, Johnny "Uncle Golden" Starks.

"Sometimes reality is too complex. Stories give it form."

Jean Luc Godard

Contents

Foreword

by Miranda, Larissa, and Gabrielle Starks

Miranda Starks

"Strolling With Stories: Tales From Horsepen" is such a special and personal book. I found myself laughing and crying as I read each story. This is my dad's voice and mind in print. This book has given us something tangible, other than photos, that we can pass down to future generations.

Our daddy was such a special person. He was creative, funny, gentle, hardworking, kind, dependable, and loving. He had a fierce love for his family, and it showed. He was a great husband, took great care of our mother, who was his best friend. I think about how he would call her to come back to his man cave, and they would sit and talk and laugh for hours. He was a great father. He had a special relationship with each of his girls; he understood each of us, and he shared and invested in each of our interests and talents.

With me, he shared his love of music and singing. We were karaoke partners, and he was excited when I started singing background for a local artist. Through that connection, we helped him realize a dream he had always had, which was to record a song he wrote: "I Must Be In Love."'

With Larissa, he shared a love of art. He was always sketching, and when he saw her natural talent, he would have her paint pictures for him and others.

With Gabrielle, they shared a love for cooking. He was always experimenting in the kitchen, sometimes unsuccessfully, but they would have cooking competitions every year.

And last but not least, he shared a love of history and writing with Jessica. He kept a notebook filled with stories and songs he wrote. He also loved genealogy, and he and Jessica would sit and talk about family and create stories together. Now, she is the family genealogist and author. Her first work, The Lynching Calendar, is a result of the love of history, and now, she is sharing with you the stories he created about his beloved Horsepen, the place he grew up in Gore Springs, MS.

He would be so excited to see his stories in print. I am so thankful that Jessica has taken the time to write these stories out. I pray you enjoy reading these quirky tales that our daddy used to tell. He was truly one of a kind. Good job, daddy and "Onion."

****

Larissa Starks

There is so much I could say about my dad, but that would be another book, and I'm not a writer! I can remember just sitting around doing nothing o just walking into the house only to be met with, "Hey! Did I tell you about "so and so?" They were from Horsepen!" He would say it with a sly grin on his face, and we would smile and roll our eyes, not knowing where he was going with his stories. This book gave those moments back to me; I could literally hear him saying the words as I read the pages. I held his hand as he took his last breath, something I will never forget. So much of me went with him that day.

My dad didn't have favorites between my sisters and me, but I was that one strong-willed, independent, but sickly at times and fragile - probably the one who gave him most of his gray hairs, but I always knew he had my back.

I miss him more than I can put into words, but this book brings him back and gives people a glimpse of parts of him that they didn't know even existed.

Thank you, Jupee (as we call her), for writing this book and giving our daddy back to us for a moment.

****

Gabrielle Starks

I never thought about how challenging it must have been for our father to raise four girls with very different personalities. He had a different relationship with each of us.

One of my favorite memories of my dad was us sitting in the living room watching classic boxing matches, then him calling me the family alcoholic but telling me he has my favorite beer out in his man cave in the same breath!

Out father was a man of a few words, and even though he never said it, one thing's for sure: daddy loved his girls, and we loved our daddy.

Preface

Writing has always been a major part of who I am since birth. I can remember my parents telling me how I used to write stories about family trips and crafting short stories to give as gifts to my sisters for their birthdays and Christmas. It wasn't until I became an adult that I realized that my love of writing was genetic. My dad, Larry Starks, was also an avid writer. He wrote poems, short stories, and songs that my family and I will forever cherish.

My dad and I never wrote down stories together, but our mutual love came together in the form of oral stories. Some days, we'd just be watching TV and come up with stories together. I'd love to egg him on to see how far he could take the story before running out of ideas.

One particular set of stories that my dad and I bonded over were his "Horsepen Stories." My dad lived in Gore Springs, MS in a community called Hosspen Road. However, you know we southerners can sometimes speak in our own language, so the road affectionately became known as Horsepen Road. This road is your standard country road - cows, trees, dirt, and gravel - but there's always been something significant and loveable about this area that people who know about it simply adore.

Dad would create these hilarious, off-the-wall stories about his old stomping ground. These stories made us laugh, scratch our heads, and smile in appreciation. I hope they do the same for you.

Disclaimer

This is a work of fiction. The authors in no way represent the companies, corporations, or brands mentioned in this book. The likeness of historical/famous figures has been used fictitiously; the author does not speak for or represent these people. All opinions expressed in this book are the authors' or fictional.

In no way, shape, or form are any of these stories factual, nor should they be considered factual, unless otherwise noted. All people, events, television shows, and anything else mentioned are not connected to Horsepen in any way, shape, or form. All of these stories are purely for fun.

Prologue

"Another Saturday," I thought to myself. "Another Saturday traveling down this road." I was miserable as I stared out the back of my dad's Ford F-150, gazing at the endless highway that leads to Horsepen.

Horsepen is a small Mississippi community where my dad grew up and my family still lives. Horsepen was the kind of town that most people assume all Southern states are like: dirt roads, cows, trees, and zero cell service. Just your classic, country community.

Don't get me wrong, I loved seeing my family, and I appreciated being able to visit the land that my granddaddy worked so hard to purchase and keep in our family, I just HATED the drive! But, my dad said that we can't forget Horsepen, so every Saturday, my mom and I got in the car and took the miserable trip with my dad to Horsepen.

When we finally made it, we did our usual thing: everyone gets out of the truck and greets the family (and random old men who came by for a beer and a good laugh with my uncles), my mom and I go inside and talk with my aunts and other women inside the house, my dad comes in to speak to the women and then heads back outside to drink, talk, sometimes barbecue, and listen to music with the men. And we followed this usual routine for the first few hours of the trip until my dad decided to switch things up on me a little bit. "Onion," dad said to me as he walked inside the house, "Come on, let's go for a walk."

My dad was a taciturn man, and he didn't say much of anything unless he had something he felt was worth saying. I, being naturally quiet and terse like him, was totally caught off guard by this sudden request. Two quiet people walking on a country road on a random evening? I wasn't sure if I was in trouble, he wanted us to exercise more, or if he was going to whack me and leave me under the nearby bridge like my uncle did his car years prior. But I got up anyway, interested to see what this walk would turn into.

And so we began. We walked down my granddaddy's long, dusty driveway and started on the rock-covered path of the road. The first couple minutes of our walk was fairly quiet, the sound of crushed rocks colliding with our shoes and dad's casual sips of Miller High Life breaking the expected silence between us.

After a few more quiet moments, my dad started. "Onion, I know our trips down here aren't exactly the most exciting part of your weekend, but I want you to really understand why our trips down here are so important."

"I know you don't want us to forget about Horsepen and where we came from, dad. I completely understand." I didn't want him to think that I didn't appreciate him bringing us here and having us around our family.

"Yeah that's true, and I'm glad you know that, but I don't know if you quite understand just how rich our history is and how you and your sisters can continue that legacy. And since you've been doing our family history, I think now is the right time to fill you in on some history."

"What do you mean, dad?"

"Come on," my dad said, grinning at me with his gap on full display. "I have a few things to show you."

1

The Stygian Bridge

So, my dad and I continued our walk. A few minutes down the road was an old, rickety, wooden bridge. This bridge had been in Horsepen for decades - you could tell. It was always frightening to cross because it never felt fully secure and you could easily see the 10-foot drop into muddy, swampy water underneath. Nonetheless, the residents of Horsepen managed to face their fears and cross over this bridge every single day.

Dad stopped right at the bridge, to my relief. " Do you know the name of this bridge?"

"Umm...The Horsepen Bridge?"

Dad let out a slight laugh as he puffed his Newport 100 cigarette. "It's called the Stygian Bridge. This bridge is important because it's how our family got to Horsepen."

"Really?" I was intrigued now.

"Your great great granddaddy escaped to freedom by hiding under this very bridge."

I couldn't believe it! Our own piece of history! "He escaped from slavery under this bridge?"

"Well....not exactly," dad chuckled. He escaped his first wife by telling her he was going to the well to get some water. Instead of going to the well, he left the bucket in the front yard and walked 30 miles to this bridge. He decided to hide out for a few days to make sure she didn't find him, and he eventually settled here, remarried your great great grandmama, and started another family. If it weren't for that second family, we wouldn't be here!"

"So...papa was a rolling stone?" I joked.

"Kinda, yeah," dad chuckled.

"...okay, dad." I laughed.

"I got more to show you, Onion. Let's keep going."

2

Horsepilantis

I was ready to continue our walk, but I still had questions about the Stygian bridge. "But Dad, how did he make it under the bridge all that time? How did he eat and where did he sleep? Was he that desperate to get away for his first wife?"

"Oh, I forgot to mention that part!" Dad took another sip of beer and another puff of his cigarette, dropping ashes on his favorite plaid blue shirt.

I'll admit, he had me locked in at this moment. I thought he had a real explanation for me.

"Ever heard of Atlantis?"

"...yea...?" I had no idea where he was going with this.

"Well, under that bridge was the lost city! Atlantis was actually a small part of the city of Horsepelantis. Most folks don't know that part of the story, though. He didn't know about it until he escaped and hid under the bridge that it existed.

"Horse...pilantis?" And to think, I was really trying to take him seri-ously....

That's right! It was a big, bustling Black town, like Tulsa, Oklahoma, in its time. They had all kinds of shops, great food, excellent music, and they didn't really have much crime. It was really the ideal place to live. He was able to stay there and live in the city for a while so he could hide out. He almost stayed there permanently, but you know, when it started going underwater, he thought it might be best to head on his way. That's when he came on to Horsepen - this part above the bridge was the lucky section that never sunk!" After finishing his explanation, he just stopped and grinned at me.

"Umm...." I shook my head. "Well, if you say so."

"You didn't ask me what happened to the people, Onion!"

"....What happened to the people, dad?"

"Why, I'm glad you asked! To escape the city, almost the entire population left for Mars. But, a select few were left behind."

"Who was left behind, dad?"

"Red Hot the Troublemaker, Big Duck the Peacemaker, Bristle Hound the Dog Caller, and Cornbread the Bread Maker!" Dad's amusement seeped through his nose and spread through his broad shoulders. I was tickled too because the "select few" he mentioned were the nicknames of my Uncle Marvin, my dad, Uncle James, and Uncle Cornbread, respectively.

4

"Now come on! I got more to show you before it gets dark!"

3

Horsepen's Monarchy

As we marched on to our next landmark, dad decided to fill me in on some more Horsepen history. "Did you know that Horsepen used to have its own government, too?"

"It did?"

"Yep! Horsepen used to be a monarchy! Had its own king and a queen! It was slightly modeled after Horsepilantis' setup, you know."

Something about what he said to me didn't sit right in my spirit. But, I decided to see what he was going to say anyway. "Dad, what are you talking about?"

Dad's big eyes jotted out into the distance as if he was trying to think. "King Plum, Queen Blackberria,...." His eyes suddenly turned towards me to see my astonished look on my face. His belly was shaking so hard; he could barely hold in his laughter.

"Now wait a–"

"- And Prince Horseapple!" Dad burst into a deep belly laugh. He laughed about it so hard; he spilled some of his Miller on the grit below.

I couldn't believe him, and I was torn! On the one hand, I was impressed that he came up with such out-of-pocket names so quickly; however, I couldn't believe he would pull something like that out of his back pocket and tell it to me with such ease! Who was this man?!

All I could do was shake my head and keep walking.

"What?!" He paused, still laughing. "Don't you believe me, Onion?"

4

Crazy Mule

Once dad caught up to me again, we continued down the aged road. By this time, we were only about half a mile away from the Stygian Bridge, but there were so many different things I was starting to see that I had never noticed before, including an antiquated house on the left side of the road, hidden behind some trees and brush.

It was a simple home, probably no more than one or two rooms. You could tell that it had been abandoned for a number of years and gradually worn down by the continuation of time and lack of care. Tattered white paint covered the quaint house, and what once was a strong and sturdy roof was now a caved-in cluster of wood on top of the house. Shards of dusty glass surrounded the windows and vines were now wrapping themselves around the windowsills.

"Dad, whose house was that?"

He paused and smiled at me, as he adjusted his Steelers cap. I knew he had a story for this one too.

"You've heard of Crazy Horse, haven't you?" My dad was a huge history buff and made sure my sisters and I learned as much as possible.

"Yeah. Native American leader, right? Helped to preserve tribal land?"

"Right! Well, Did you know his great grandfather was born here?"

"Oh really? What was his name?"

"Crazy Mule!"

Again, we both started laughing. He was always coming up with something!

"I'm for real!" He laughed. "Just like Crazy Horse, Crazy Mule wanted to make sure that Horsepen's culture and history were preserved, and that no one got in the way of that. If anyone got out of line or tried to do anything crazy, Crazy Mule would grab his scabbage and yell-"

"Wait, what's a scabbage?" I was thoroughly confused.

"You know, a scabbage, you hold your knife in it. The old folks used to have them and they called them that...I don't know."

"Oh...okay then." I shrugged.

The word didn't sound familiar to me, so I just went with it. I later learned that what he was trying to say was "scabbard," which is a kind of holder for a weapon, like a gun or a knife.

"-but Crazy Mule would grab his scabbage, and yell his war cry, "Ep

Here!" and run them out of town!

5

Dancing At The Juke Joint

We walked a few more minutes down the road and came up to an old building where one of my uncles worked called The Rusty Roof.

The Rusty Roof was an unassuming place, old and worn. It looked like your typical, abandoned country building during the day. However, when night fell, the metal shack turned into one of the hottest nightclubs around. But why were we here? What did this place have to do with Horsepen's history?

Here came that gapped grin again.

"You know that show you and your mama like to watch? "Dancing With The Stars?"

"....yeah...?" I thought to myself, "I know he isn't about to make a connection...."

"Did you know that they took the idea for that show from Horsepen? of course, we didn't get any credit or money for it, but it started right there in that building."

"Please explain." I never could understand how dad could come up with this stuff.

"Yep, sure did. Except here it was called, 'Dancing at the Juke Joint.'"

"Dancing at the-....wow, dad. Wow." I snickered.

"It was later renamed 'Dancing At The Bar,' but the big folks in Holly-wood changed it again for TV, don't you know," taking another sip of his Miller.

"All the best dancers from around Horsepen used to come once a year to dance for the judges and see who would be crowned Horsepen's best. One of Odaefus' sons and his girlfriend actually won the first contest."

What was his name?

"Onaephus," he quickly answered back.

I couldn't help but let out a quick snicker before asking my next question. "What was his girlfriend's name?

"....Louise." I almost tripped him up, but he recovered well, but I was still slightly disappointed.

"Louise? You come up with Onaefus Starks...and Louise?"

Dad just couldn't stop laughing. "Well, I don't know...that was her name, Onion. Stop asking questions!" he mumbled, jokingly.

6

Soul Tunnel

I thought he had let go of that epic dance tale, but he had one more detail to include that would absolutely blow my mind.

"You know, Onion, they invented a popular dance the year they won, too. Know what it was?"

"What was it?"

"The Soul Tunnel."

"The Soul Tunnel? What dance is that?"

"That was the first Soul Train Line. Don Cornelius was one of the judges that year and took the idea with him when he created Soul Train. That's how it started being called The Soul Train Line."

I decided to egg him on a little bit. "Did they win a trophy too?"

"Naw," dad said. "But they did win a year supply of moonshine!"

By this point, I was convinced that my dad had truly lost his mind.

"What?!" He joked. "Laugh all you want, Onion – you're gonna find out I'm telling the truth one of these days!"

7

Six

I thought we were ready to move on from my dad's jocular history of The Rusty Roof, but he had one more anecdote for me connected to the local gem.

"Did I ever tell you how I got the nickname, 'Six,' Onion?"

"Naw, don't believe you have."

"Well, when I was young and had good knees, I used to run up and down these roads all the time. Folks would try to race me, but I was always too fast for 'em. But, one particular night set my name in stone." Dad opened the front pocket on his shirt to pull out his lighter and Newports to light up another cigarette.

"What happened?"

"Well, one night me and my cousin Danny went to The Rusty Roof with my other cousin Mack. He left early, and we didn't have a car, so we wound up having to walk back to the house that night. But we were used to walking, so we thought it wouldn't be much different from any other night."

"Right....?"

"Well, we got right over by where Crazy Mule's house was, and Danny heard something rustling in the bushes on the side of the house. We both looked around and didn't see nothing, so we kept on walking."

"Uh, huh..." I was getting into this story.

"We walked down a little further, and I felt a rock hit me on my shoulder. We looked around again, still didn't see nothing. So we decided to walk a little faster. A little further down the path, another rock hits me in the back. We turn around and see this large figure jump out the bushes and yell, 'YAAA!' So we took off running!"

"I know you were gone!" I chimed in.

"Sho' was!" Dad laughed. "I ran so fast, all I could hear was Danny yelling from behind me, 'wait! Wait for me! Don't leave me!' But I wasn't trying to hear it! We had about a mile left to get to my house, but I got there in 10 seconds that night!"

"Did y'all ever find out who or what it was in the bushes that night?"

"Yeah! It turned out it was Mack who scared us!"

"What?! How did he know y'all were out there?" He had me hooked.

"To this day, I don't know, Onion. But the next day, he came to my house and asked, "Y'all were running pretty fast out there last night, weren't you?" When he told us it was him, we all couldn't help but laugh about it. That was a significant emotional event!" Dad's guffaw intermingled with the smoke from his newly lit Newport. Dad's favorite term for something that scared him or made him nervous was "Significant emotional event."

"But anyway, Mack told me, 'You were running like The Six Million Dollar Man, fella!' And that's where my nickname Six came from." *The Six Million Dollar Man* was a TV show in the '70s about a man who had superhuman strength, speed, and other powers that helped him fight crime and defeat the bad guys.

Note: My dad didn't make this story up – it was actually a real thing that happened!

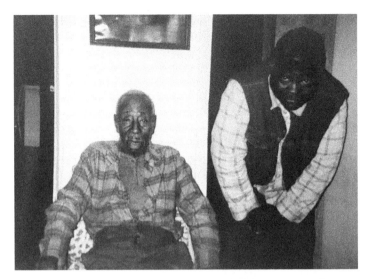

8

HASA

As we finished laughing at his seventh tall tale, we realized that it was starting to get dark. "I remember walking and running miles out here at night," said dad. "I'm too old to be stuck out here when the lights go out. Let's head on back to the house!"

So off we went, back down that old, gravel road towards my grandaddy's house. I'll admit, one neat thing about living outside of the city is that you have a full, uninterrupted view of the sky. Lost in my thoughts, my dad suddenly brought me back to reality. "Look, Onion! A shooting star!" I never really seen one before. It was so vivid, so beautiful.

"Speaking of the stars, did you know NASA actually started in Horsepen?"

Oh, Lord...here we go again...

"..It was actually first called HASA-"

"-did it mean the same thing, dad?" I thought I'd test the waters since he seemed to be so into this story. For those who don't know, NASA stands for National Aeronautics and Space Administration.

"Yeah! Horsepen Astronauts and Space Aviation!" he laughed. "Wait...is that what that stands for?"

"...no, dad," all I could do was chuckle at him.

"Well, you know what I mean!" he laughed.

I thought that was all there was to that story, but boy, was I wrong.

9

Cousin Odaefus

"Anyway," dad continued, "HASA was there first, and they sent the very first astronaut into space, and he was one of our relatives."

"Our relative? What relative?"

"Odaefus Starks." I've never seen dad grin so big in my life. His smile was so big, the shine from his teeth lit up the road in front of us. "He was my dad's-aunt's-niece's-brothers'-father's-nephew son."

"Oh wow," I chimed in. It's a wonder you can remember all that." I decided to tease a little bit. "I'm not sure I caught that....can you repeat that lineage for me?"

"Uhh...." my dad started. "dad's-aunt's-cousin's-nephew's.....oh stop it!" He laughed!

"One day, they were just supposed to send him up there for a test launch in the first spaceships, which they originally called Scuttle Buttles."

"Scuttle Buttles?"

"That's right, that's right." Dad started. "They are now known as space shuttles."

"Oh goodness..."

"But anyway, they shot him up there to space, but he got stuck on the moon. He shouted, 'HASA, HASA, bring me back down!' but they never could get to him. So, he was just stuck up there, trying to figure out how to get back home and yelling to HASA to get back to earth."

"Shame, shame," I chimed in. "Did he ever get back home?"

"Nope. As a matter of fact, they got so tired of hearing him call for HASA that the program moved away and changed their name to NASA.

"Just an injustice." There was no point in fighting him anymore. We were in too deep.

"Yes, yes it is. But now, he travels through space, continuing to explore the great unknown. And sometimes, he'll fly by on a shooting star to say hello. Sometimes, if you look REALLY close, you'll see him waving from the moon!"

10

Star Track

We were inching closer and closer back to my grandaddy's house, but dad still had one more Sci-Fi story to throw at me.

"Speaking of Odaephus and outer space, Horsepen never did get credit for Star Track." Dad was referring to one of his favorite TV shows, *Star Trek*, but....we're in the South, so it's Star Track.

"What do you mean, dad?"

"Well, you know we couldn't have HASA without a few stories. And one of the original members of HASA took some of those stories and went to Hollywood with them and sold them....Star Track."

"Just a shame," I added.

"Ain't it? Hey, you know what their phrase was?"

"It was 'Live Long and Prosper,' wasn't it?"

"Naw! Hollywood changes things, you know. It was actually 'Live Long and Grow Collard Greens,'" the statement spewed out of his mouth with laughter mixed in.

"Oh my gosh....Dad!" I had no words. I just covered my face and laughed. Who else comes up with stuff like this?! What is wrong with my father?!

"What, Onion?! One of these days you're gonna find out I was telling you real Horsepen history! You'll see one day!"

11

Horsepen University

By this point, I found myself suddenly getting more and more into these Horsepen tales. "So dad...how exactly did they learn about Science and start HASA? Was there a school around here at one point?"

"Why, of course!" Dad said in a dramatic hiss. "Horsepen University was one of the highest-rated learning institutions in Mississippi!"

"Oh, was it?"

"It was better than Yale and Harvard combined in its heyday. Many amazing scientists and scholars came out of Horsepen University!"

"Well then," I responded. "You learn something new every day."

NOTE: My late, great uncle Johnny Golden Starks actually confirmed that my dad was telling the truth, to an extent. He told us that there actually used to be a school in Horsepen, and my dad ate that information up!

12

Lou Gossiper

"Hey Onion, you know something else? We had a famous actor come out of Horsepen too?"

"Do I know this actor?"

"Yeah! This guy's been in all kinds of stuff we've watched - *The Jeffersons*, *Bonanza*, *Good Times*, and *Roots*!"

"Really? Which actor?" I wasn't sure why I got excited, but I did.

"Lou Gossett, Jr.!"

"What? Lou Gossett, Jr.?!"

"Yeah!" I could tell dad was excited I was going along with it. "But most people don't know that Gossett isn't his real last name."

"What is it?"

"Gossiper."

"Wait...let me get this straight." I was already tickled. "So you mean to tell me that Lou Gossett, Jr.'s real name is Lou Gossiper, Jr.?"

"Sho 'nuff," Dad said, so serious. "When he got his big break, the executives in Hollywood told him that name wouldn't fly, so he shortened it to Gossett."

"I see.."

My dad, my dad...

I had no idea that years later, my mom and I would have a chance to meet Lou Gossett, Jr., and snap a photo with him!

13

Rick James, Homeboy

I could tell we had almost made it back to my Grandaddy's house because I could smell barbecue in the air and hear the faint sound of music in the distance. If we did nothing else in Horsepen, we had a barbecue and listened to music.

"Dad, what song is that?" The tune sounded familiar to me, but I just couldn't catch it.

"That's *Mary Jane* by Rick James," dad answered as he started singing along with the song. Dad was a karaoke junkie and would sing all the classics in his own unique style.

"That's right! I thought it sounded familiar!"

"Speaking of Rick James-"

"Aw, Lawd," I thought to myself.

"-did you know he was from Horsepen too?"

"...was he, dad?"

"Yeah! You didn't know? Before he left and made it big, he and his group were popular around here. At first, they were called Rick James and the Gravel Road Band, but when they made it big, it was changed to Rick James and the Stone City Band."

We had made it to the driveway at this point, but he still had another story to tell...

14

The Quiets

As we walked our final stretch, the song switched to *It's a Love Thing*.

"You know who this group is, Onion?"

"The...Whispers?"

"That's right! They were Horsepen too, don't you know?"

"Let me guess - they underwent a name change too?"

"Sho' did! They used to be called the Quiets!"

We both burst into laughter as we finally reached the front yard. "I don't know if I can take any more history for the day; I'm going in the house!"

"Okay," dad laughed. "Now, listen - don't forget your Horsepen history! It's important! Be sure to keep it alive!"

"I won't forget!" I giggled as I headed into the house.

I never did.

And I never will.

Afterword

I hope you have enjoyed reading these stories as much as I loved retelling them! Again, NONE of these stories are true - these are all tall tales my dad made up to make me smile (though we were all shocked when we found out about the school!).

The memories attached to these stories are some of my favorites with my dad that I will cherish forever. Although he is no longer here with me, I know that his legacy and spirit will live forever through Horsepen and through these stories he told me.

So here's to you, dad: Larry Starks, one of my best friends, my biggest cheerleaders, and my first love. I hope I did your stories justice. Be sure to tell Cousin Odaefus "Hi" for me!

Love,
  Onion

Acknowledgments

To Bernard Harrell, thank you for being such a wonderful and devoted friend to my dad and for always being there for my mom and my sisters. We appreciate you more than you know.

To Roosevelt and Peggy Hankins, thank you guys for always providing laughs, love, and support throughout the years. I know dad and Buck are having a great time together in Heaven.

To Solomon and Amiyah, thank you both for bringing so much light and love to our family. You both inspire me to keep pushing to achieve my dreams so I can make it easier for you both to achieve yours. I know you are both destined for greatness and I'll be there with you both, every step of the way. I'm honored to be your aunt.

To current and future Starks descendants, please know that we come from a line of strong, resilient people. I am proud to be a Starks, and I hope you all are too.

Notes

Chapter 3

Crazy Horse - Also named *Tasunke Witco*, was born a member of the Oglala Band of Lakota Sioux in or near the Black Hills of South Dakota. Crazy Horse was actually called Curley Hair as a boy, during a battle As a young boy Crazy Horse was known as Curley Hair. Later he was renamed Horse On Sight. During a battle with another group of Native Americans, he showed such bravery that his father, who was originally named Crazy Horse, gave his name to his son in honor of his bravery. He was a well-respected warrior by his mid-teens and went on to be affiliated with some of the most significant campaigns, battles, and resistance efforts by the Lakota against the United States Government, who aimed to force American Indians to reservations. In 1877, Crazy Horse attempted to attack Colonel Nelson Miles' force, in one last attempt of resistance. Unfortunately, the attack was not successful and Crazy Horse was forced to surrender. He died on September 5, 1877. Crazy Horse was also known to refuse to take photos or have his likeness recorded. He believed that taking a photo would cause his life to be shortened and a part of his soul would be taken.

Sources: https://www.nps.gov/libi/learn/historyculture/crazy-horse.htm

https://crazyhorsememorial.org/story/the-history/about-crazy-hor

se-the-man

Chapter 5

Dancing With The Stars - A U.S. reality show on ABC that is based on the British television series, *Strictly Come Dancing* and follows several celebrities who are paired up with professional dancers to compete and determine who out of the group is the best dancer. The show premiered in 2005 and is still running as of the publication of this book.

Source: https://www.imdb.com/title/tt0463398/

Chapter 6

Soul Train - A music and dance television show that aired beginning in 1971 and quickly became the premier place to showcase minority artists, dancers, and music. The show was originally hosted by creator Don Cornelius, with different hosts eventually coming in as the show aged. *Soul Train* ended in 2006.

Soul Train Line - A staple of the television show, Soul Train, was The Soul Train Line. Dancers create two lines across from each other with space in the middle for dancers to glide down and perform until they reach the end of the line, signaling the turn of another dancer. "The Soul Train Line" is considered to be a spin on The Stroll, which was created in the 1950's.

Sources: https://www.imdb.com/title/tt0161194/
   https://dance.lovetoknow.com/The_Stroll_50s_Dance

Chapter 8

NASA - The National Aeronautics and Space Administration (NASA), was created in response to the Soviet space program and officially opened for business in 1958. Since its beginning, NASA has been responsible for and critical in technological progress and success in space science, aeronautics, spaceflight, aeronautics, and much much. NASA's two first high-profile projects were *Project Mercury*, which worked to find out if humans could, in fact, survive in space; and Project Gemini, which worked to perfect the necessary things needed to land a human on the Moon by the end of the 1960s. To this day, NASA continues to make innovations in space exploration.

Source: https://www.nasa.gov/content/nasa-history-overview

Chapter 9

Star Trek - An American television show created, written, and produced by Gene Roddenberry that follows the adventures of the members of the starship USS Enterprise, who are on a mission to explore space and "boldly go where no man has gone before." The series is set in the 23rd century, in a time where an alien species called the Vulcans have shared their technology with humankind, allowing humans to travel intergalactically. Due to low ratings, the show only ran from 1966-1969; however, the show immediately gained a cult following with their fans, called *Trekkies*.

Source: https://www.britannica.com/topic/Star-Trek-series-1966-196
9

Chapter 11

Lou Gossett, Jr. - An African American Emmy and Academy Award-winning actor, who starred in movies such as *A Raisin in the Sun* (1961), *Roots* (1977), and *An Officer and a Gentleman* (1982).

Source: https://www.britannica.com/biography/Louis-Gossett-Jr

Chapter 12

Rick James & The Stone City Band- Born James Johnson, Jr., Rick James was known for his unique mesh of funk, rock, R&B, and soul. The nephew of Temptations singer Melvin Franklin, Rick worked as a songwriter for Motown before becoming the household name we know him to be today. The Stone City Band, which comprised of original members Levi Ruffin, Tom Mcdermott, Lanise Hughes, Nate Hughes, and Danny Lemelle, was formed in 1977 and Rick James stepped out as a solo artist and created his own sound, called Punk Funk. They are best known for their hits such as *You and I*, *Mary Jane*, and *Bustin' Out.*

Sources: http://www.rickjames.com/bio.php
   https://open.spotify.com/artist/0MauOPW6z1oqN2aTl8qIk0#:~:text
=Considered%20by%20many%20of%20their,of%20Punk%20Funk%2
C%20Rick%20James.

Chapter 13

The Whispers - R&B group comprised of members, Walter Scott, Wallace Scott. Nicholas Caldwell, Marcus Hutson, and Gordy Harmon (later replaced by Leaveil Degree) that started in 1963 and were originally called "The Eden Trio." The Whispers became the first artists featured on SOLAR Records, then called Soul Train Records, which was co-owned by Don Cornelius. The group went on the create various hits, including *Lady, Just Gets Better With Time*, and *The Beat Goes On.*

Sources: http://www.thewhispers.com/bio/bio.html

About The Authors

Jessica Starks is a businesswoman and professional writer who enjoys expressing herself creatively. She also is a genealogist by hobby who appreciates the stories of her ancestors. When not absorbed in her writing, Jessica loves reading, cooking, watching old movies, and playing games with her family. She lives in Mississippi, surrounded by family and friends.

Larry Starks was a multifaceted husband and father, and grandfather. He loved history, writing poems and songs, telling stories, and karaoke. He loved working in his garden in his free time, restoring old cars, and playing pranks on his family members.

Also by Jessica Starks

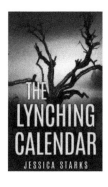

The Lynching Calendar

https://jdscribes.com/product/the-lynching-calendar

False Accusations.

Toxic Love.

Fear of the Misunderstood.

Innocence Lost.

Internal Torture that Lasts for a Lifetime.

The Lynching Calendar gives readers a sneak peek into one of America's darkest times. History tends to tell the story from one perspective, but what if we had the chance to hear the story from those involved? The Lynching Calendar allows us a chance to hear the full story and show that, no matter what the circumstance may be, there is more than one side to every story.

CPSIA information can be obtained
at www.ICGtesting.com
Printed in the USA
JSHW011812050721
16611JS00004B/40